Peppa Pig™

The Children's Fête

Peppa and her friends are at playgroup. Mr Bull is checking the school roof.

"Moo!" shouts Mr Bull. "Who put this roof on for you?"
"You did, Mr Bull," says Madame Gazelle.
Mr Bull nods. "Lovely job! It will last you a lifetime."

Madame Gazelle takes Mr Bull inside.
She points to the ceiling. It is leaking water.
"Look!" she says. "It is going drip-drip!"

"You need a new roof," says Mr Bull.

Drip!

Drip!

Drip!

"Where are we going to get the money for a new school roof?" asks Madame Gazelle.

The children have a good idea. They decide to put on a school fête to get the money for the new school roof.

It is the day of the children's fête. Danny Dog is in charge of the microphone.
"Hello, grown-ups!" he says. "Get your money out for the new school roof!"

Emily Elephant is in charge
of the bric-a-brac stall.
"Roll up, roll up," she calls.
"All sorts of bits and bobs!"

"Hmm . . ." says Mr Fox. "This all looks very interesting."

Mr Fox is always looking for bric-a-brac.

"Balloons!" shouts Pedro Pony.
"Lovely balloons!"
"May I have a red one?"
says Madame Gazelle.
"How much money have you
got?" asks Pedro.
Madame Gazelle tips all of
the coins out of her purse.

Clink!

Suzy Sheep is in
charge of the
face-painting stall.
"Can I be a mountain leopard
please?" says Miss Rabbit.
"No," says Suzy.
"I can only do fruit."

"OK," says Miss Rabbit.
"Can I be . . ."
"A plum!" decides Suzy.

Mr Bull comes to visit Peppa.
He has got a green face.
"I am an apple!" he booms.

"Would you like to try the lucky dip?" asks Peppa.
"Everyone's a winner!"

Mr Bull drops
a coin into
Peppa's tin.

Mr Bull reaches into
the lucky dip barrel. He pulls out a dolly.
"Can I have a go?" asks Mrs Cat.
Mrs Cat wins a toy digger.

"Oh!" gasps Peppa. "Do you want to swap?"
Mr Bull and Mrs Cat do not want to swap.

They are pleased with their lucky dip prizes!

Pant!
Puff!

Freddy Fox calls all the grown-ups. It is time for the mummies and daddies race. Everybody has to get into a sack and jump across the field.

"On your marks, get set . . .
GO!" shouts Freddy.

The mummies and daddies have lots of fun jumping in sacks. At the end, Madame Gazelle has an important announcement to make.

"We have raised enough money to buy a new school roof!" she cries. "Again!"